MEL BAY PRESENTS

STRING BAND CLASSICS

FIDDLE

TRANSCRIBED BY BILL GUEST

I0792708

CD Contents

1 Dance All Night [3:16]	13 Way Out There [4:15]
2 You Ain't Talking to Me [3:34]	14 Carroll County Blues [2:30]
3 Money Musk [2:48]	15 Old Jimmy Sutton [2:23]
4 There's More Pretty Girls [3:02]	16 Devilish Mary [2:59]
5 Fire on the Mountain [2:18]	17 Way Down the Old Plank Road [3:15]
6 Gypsy Girl [2:40]	18 Tater Patch [2:36]
7 Pig Ankle Rag [3:24]	19 My Dixie Darling [2:47]
8 Wild Bill Jones [3:45]	20 Free Little Bird [3:11]
9 Sleeping Lulu [3:21]	21 Been All Around This World [3:25]
10 Meeting in the Air [3:42]	22 Goodbye, Miss Liza [3:00]
11 Hawks and Eagles [2:48]	23 Lee Highway Blues [3:41]
12 Who Broke the Lock [2:52]	

Produced under license from Rounder Records Corp., One Camp Street, Cambridge, Massachusetts, 02140 U.S.A

1 2 3 4 5 6 7 8 9 0

Visit us on the Web at www.melbay.com — E-mail us at email@melbay.com

Table Of Contents

This page has been left blank
to avoid awkward page turns.

Track 1

Dance All Night

46
C D G C
51
D C D
56
G D
61
G SL D SL G
66
D G
71
D G D
76
G D G
D.S. al Fine

Track 2

You Ain't Talking to Me

Chorus
51
D
D
G
D
57
A
D
G
63
D
A
D
D.S. al Fine
Fiddle

Track 3

Money Musk

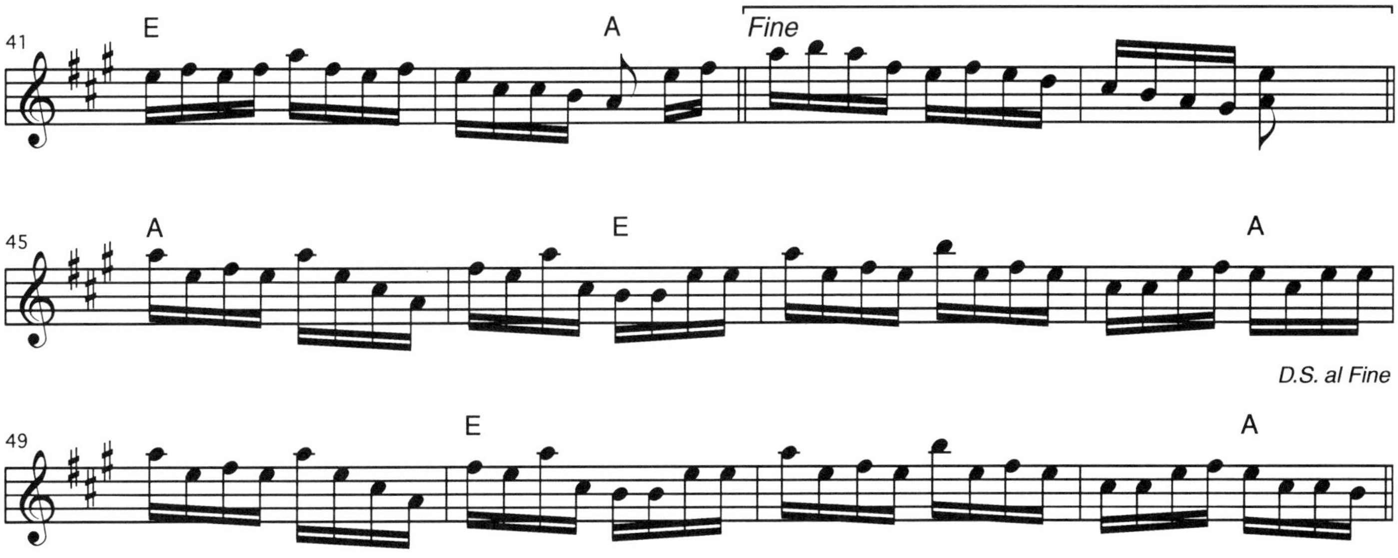
41
E
A
Fine
45
A
E
A
D.S. al Fine
49
E
A

Track 4

There's More Pretty Girls

50 A D G
55 D
60 Bm D A D Vocal
65 D A D G
70 D G
75 D Bm D A D
80 A D
85 G D G
90 D Bm D A
95 D Fiddle D D

100
G
D
105
Bm
D
110
A
D
Vocal
Fiddle
D
A
115
D
G
D
120
Bm
125
D
A
D
Vocal
D
130
A
D
G
135
D
G
D
140
Bm
D
A
D
Fiddle
Fine
Last time only
D.S. al Fine

This page has been left blank
to avoid awkward page turns.

Track 5

Fire on the Mountain

41
E
A
45
D
48
A
D
51
A
D
A
54
1, 2
E
A
Many Repeats
3
A
E
A

Track 6

Gypsy Girl

Fiddle
D.S. al Fine
last time
to Fine

Track 7

Pig Ankle Rag

C
A7 D
D D G
D B7 E9 A 1.D 2.D
D A7
D A
D G D B7 E A
D E A7 D
A7 D G
D B7 E A D A7
D A7 D
G D B7 E7 A D
SL

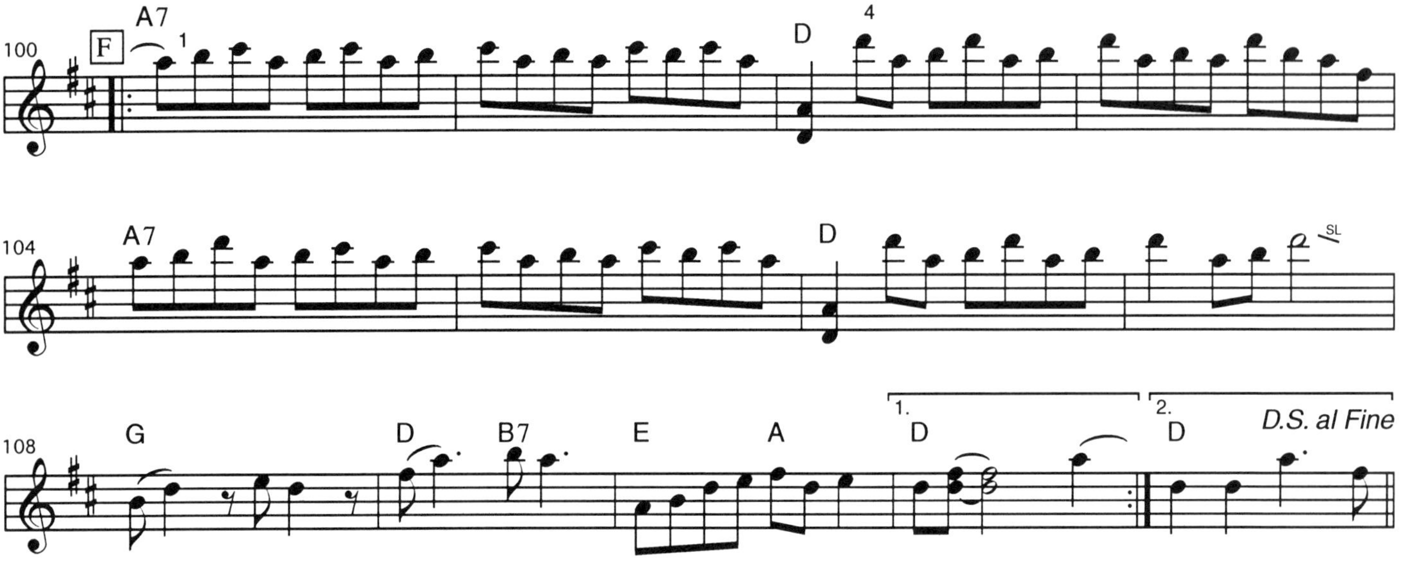
100
F
A7
D
104
A7
D
SL
108
G
D
B7
E
A
1.
D
2.
D
D.S. al Fine

This page has been left blank
to avoid awkward page turns.

Track 8

Wild Bill Jones

59
E
64
A
1, 2, 3, 4
Last verse (#5)
69
E
A
SL
76
E
A
84
E
88
A
94
E
A
Fiddle
3
A

Track 9

Sleeping Lulu

Track 10

Meeting in the Air

A
E
A
D
A
B
E
A
1st time only
A
Fine
Guitar & Fiddle Solo
A
E
A
SL
A
D
A
E
A
Vocal
A

120
E
127
A
134
140
E
148
A
154
D
160
A
B7
E
A
D.C. al Fine

Track 11

Hawks and Eagles

Track 12

Who Broke the Lock

Track 13

Way Out There

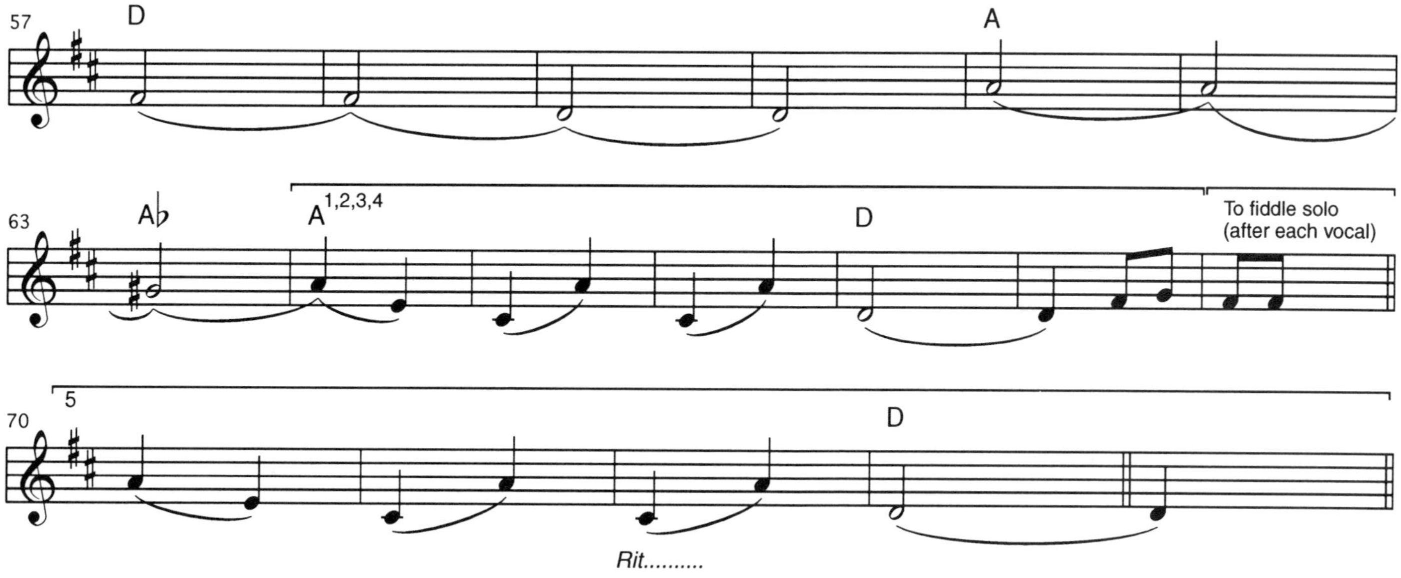
57
D
A
63
A♭
A 1,2,3,4
D
To fiddle solo
(after each vocal)
70
5
D
Rit..........

Track 14

Carroll County Blues

Guitar
3 beats
A
D
A
E
A
D
A
E
A
A
Bounce
Bow
Arco
A
D
A
E
A

99
104
D
A
E
109
A
A Keep repeating last two bars til fade out to Fine
Fine

This page has been left blank
to avoid awkward page turns.

Track 15

Old Jimmy Sutton

51
56
A
D
61
D
A
D
D
66
1, 2
3, 4
5
SL

Track 16

Devilish Mary

Last time to Fine
51
D
G
Vocal
57
62
D
67
1, 2, 3, 4, 5
G
D.
Fine

Track 17

Way Down the Old Plank Road

61
A
D
66
A
D
Fiddle D
71
A
D
A
76
D
81
A
D
86
A
D
91
A
D
Vocal
96
101
A
D
106
A
D
Vocal

A
D
D
Fiddle
A
D
A
D
Vocal/Fiddle/etc. to Fine
A
D
A
Fine
D

This page has been left blank
to avoid awkward page turns.

Track 18

Tater Patch

41
A
D
45
A
E
A
E
49
A
E
A
E
Sl
53
A
E
57
1, 2, 3, 4, 5
A
Tag on last time
E
A

Track 19

My Dixie Darling

65
D
G
Fiddle
G
73
D
G
80
D
G
D
G
87
D
92
G
98
D
G
SL
Vocal
G
105
D
113
D
G
Fiddle

Track 20

Free Little Bird

58
D
G
C
63
D
1,2,3
G
To Vocal
68
4

Track 21

Been All Around This World

70
A D G D G
76
D A D
83
A D G D G
90
D A D
D.C.

Track 22

Goodbye, Miss Liza

as performed by Highwoods Stringband

Arranged by
Bill Guest

51 D G
57 G C G D7
63 G D G Fiddle C
69 D G C
75 G D G D G
81 G Vocal C G
87 D G
93 G D G A
99 D G C
105 D G C

111 G D7 G D G Fiddle
117 C G D
123 G C
129 D G
134 D G Vocal C D
141 G C G D7
147 G D G Fiddle G D7 G D7 G

Track 23

Lee Highway Blues

49
A
D
A
D
54
D
SL
59
G
65
D
SL
SL
75
SL
83
A
D
88
A
D
A
D
93
A
D
98
1, 2, 3
D.
4
A
D